TOO MUCH PICNIC

Peter Jan Honigsberg

Illustrated by

Ryan Jones

In memory of Fred and Anne Adelberg

PJH

In memory of Gregory C. Bittel

Dedicated to Joanie, Larry and Adam Jones

RLJ

Too Much Picnic

Jazzie Bunny Press
P.O. Box 5458
Berkeley, CA. 94705

email: jazziebunnypress@yahoo.com

Copyright 2006 by Peter Jan Honigsberg
All Rights Reserved

Library of Congress Catalog Card Number: 2005937399

ISBN 1-57143-154-3

Distributed by Jazzie Bunny Press and RDR Books.

Printed in Canada

TOO MUCH PICNIC

Peter Jan Honigsberg

Illustrated by

Ryan Jones

Cocoa Mole tunnels up from his home, carrying a tray of wiggle-worm sandwiches and beetle crackers. He is on his way to the community picnic.

As Cocoa Mole digs, he thinks, "Since nobody likes these things but me, I'll get to eat them *all* by myself."

"Then, I'll join the others and eat their delicious food.

Yum, Yum, Yum.

I can't wait to stuff myself."

Everyone is coming with a favorite dish to share.

Jazzie Bunny and her mom bake their famous carrot cake.

Papa Squirrel brings a box of Crunchy O's and some donuts.

Each of the Raccoon children carries a finger bowl while Father Raccoon makes freshly squeezed lemonade.

The Possum family brings blackberries picked this morning and Mother Fox brings homemade cream.

Ms. Beaver decorates the picnic with pretty bouquets of water lilies.

Everyone is hungry and ready to eat. Cocoa Mole rushes to the head of the line. The others politely line up behind him.

When they have filled their plates, all the animals but Cocoa sit around in a large community circle.

While the elders are telling stories about the olden days, Cocoa sneaks back to the picnic for seconds and then thirds.
"I hope nobody notices," he says to himself.

Cocoa Mole can barely see over the top of his plate as he reaches for a couple slices of Mr. Fox's wild mushroom pizza, another helping of Mama Squirrel's nut bread, and two more scoops of homemade cream.

"I need to finish all this quickly, so I can go back for more," he thinks.

"After all, why should I stop eating just because I'm full?"

When it's time for dessert, Cocoa rushes off to the cake and cuts himself a really big piece.

"Whew," thinks Cocoa, "that was lucky. I was so busy eating, I almost didn't notice that it was time for dessert."

Shortly after, the children run off to play on the Daredevil Mud Slide, while Cocoa challenges Otis on the bouncing seesaw.

Soon, Cocoa must stop playing. His belly aches.

"Oh, no" Cocoa Mole moans and groans.

"I'm so stuffed. I ate too much. "

around him. Four carry yummy crunchy munchies.

"It's Too Much Picnic time," they cry in unison.

Monkey Do carries high-to-the-sky stacks of blueberry, strawberry, and banana pancakes with barrels of maple syrup and tubs of butter, singing,

"Stuff your mouth, stuff it again.
The more you eat, the more you can."

"And what about dessert?" poses Monkey Nose. He unveils chocolate-cream cakes the size of beach balls, vats of rainbow-colored ice cream, mounds of chocolate-jelly cookies, and dozens and dozens of white-glazed, chocolate-gooey,

and custard-filled donuts, all the while tempting,

"Eat this, eat that, don't suck your thumb.
Swallow it all in your tummy, tum, tum."

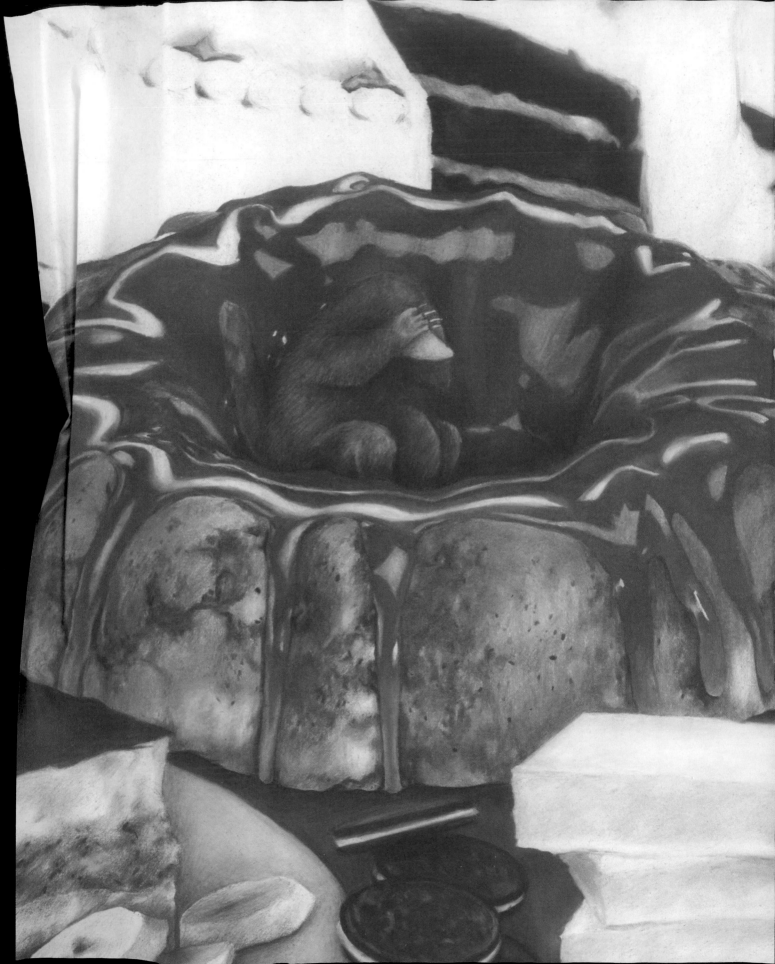

"Feast on these," Monkey See pleads as he balances trays overflowing with heaps of double cheeseburgers, monster french fries, buckets of crispy fried chicken, oodles of noodles, jumbo tacos, and supersize nachos with gobs of guacamole and cheese.

Monkey Toes brings plates of giant meatballs and spaghetti, slippery shells of colored pasta and tasty bowls of macaroni and cheese, chanting,

"Eat as much as you can, and then eat more.
Eat 'til your belly flops to the floor."

The Munchie Monkeys whirl their platters as they frolic and chant, drawing closer and closer to Cocoa Mole. Faster and faster they babble and twirl.

But no matter how hard they try to tempt him, Cocoa Mole seals his lips tightly shut. He is too stuffed to eat another thing!

As last, worn out by Cocoa's resistance, the Munchie Monkeys spin around once more and vanish.

The bright warm sun feels good as Cocoa Mole wakes up.
He misses his friends.

"I could have played with my friends instead of sleeping,
if only I had not stuffed myself," he laments.

Suddenly, he hears a moan. It's Otis Mouse.
"I ate too much, I ate too much," groans the mouse.

Cocoa Mole comforts him. "I know just how you feel, Otis."
Jazzie Bunny hops over to Cocoa Mole and Otis.

Cocoa Mole lies down on his blanket and falls asleep.
He journeys into the world of dreams.

Out of nowhere, Munchie Monkeys appear and dance feverishly

"Would you like to sit with
us in the community circle?" she asks.
"We're telling lots of funny stories."

"I'd love to join you. I was so full that I missed out on
all the fun," says Cocoa.

As Cocoa and Otis take their places in the circle, Ms. Beaver passes
around a plate of double-chocolate chip cookies. "No, thank you"
says Cocoa politely. "But I would love one of Jazzie Bunny's carrots,
if she doesn't mind. And when it's my turn to tell a story, I have a
fantastic tale to tell," Cocoa continues.

"It's all about Munchie Monkeys and Too Much Picnic."